**FRIENDS
OF ACPL**

COLOR DANCE

ANN JONAS

Greenwillow Books · New York

For my favorite
dance troupe,
Doninamy

Copyright © 1989 by Ann Jonas
All rights reserved. No part of this
book may be reproduced or utilized
in any form or by any means,
electronic or mechanical,
including photocopying,
recording or by any information
storage and retrieval system,
without permission in writing
from the Publisher,
Greenwillow Books, a division of
William Morrow & Company, Inc.,
105 Madison Avenue,
New York, N.Y. 10016.
Printed in Hong Kong by
South China Printing Co.
First Edition
10 9 8 7 6 5 4 3 2 1

Library of Congress
Cataloging-in-Publication Data
Jonas, Ann. Color dance.
Summary:
Four dancers show how colors
combine to create different colors.
[1. Color—Fiction.
2. Dancing—Fiction] I. Title.
PZ7.J664Co 1989 [E]
88-5446
ISBN 0-688-05990-2
ISBN 0-688-05991-0 (lib. bdg.)

Watercolor paints were used
for the full-color art.
The text type is Futura Bold.

S T O P

There is more than one red.
The red in this book is
the red of the rainbow and
the red used in full-color
printing. It is just as real
a red as fire engine red, apple
red, or stoplight red. It is
the essential red to use for
making clear secondary colors.

This is our dance.

Red

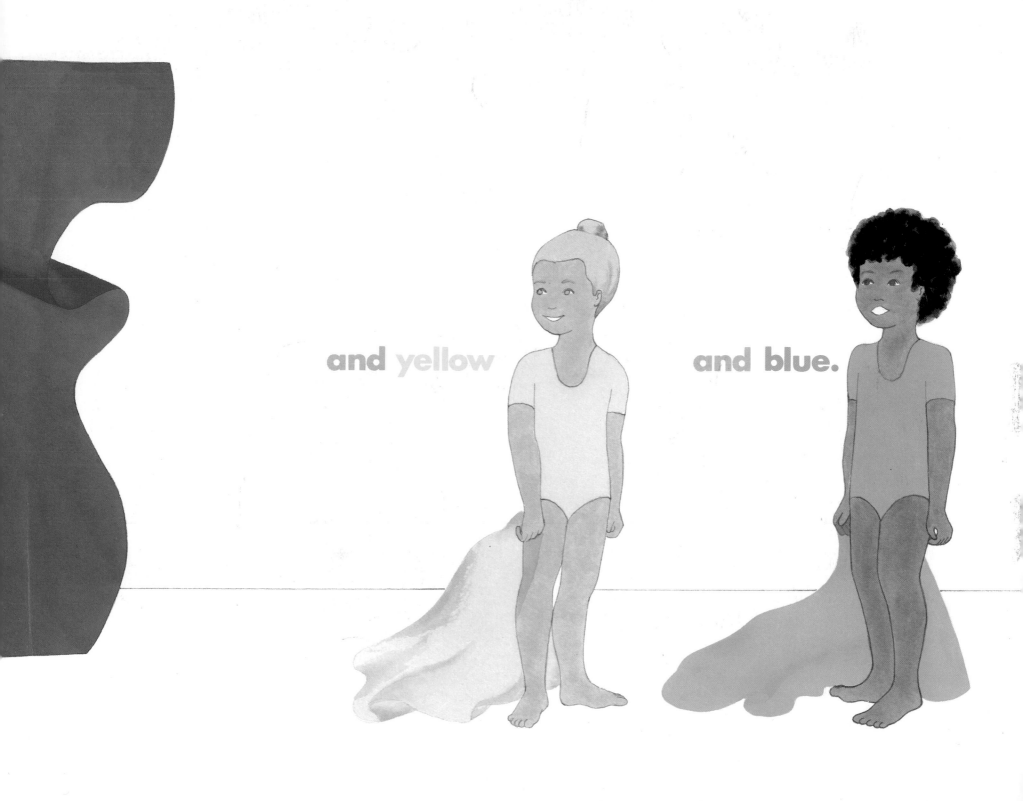

and yellow   and blue.

Orange is **red** and **yellow** mixed together.

No blue.

Green is yellow and blue mixed together.

No red.

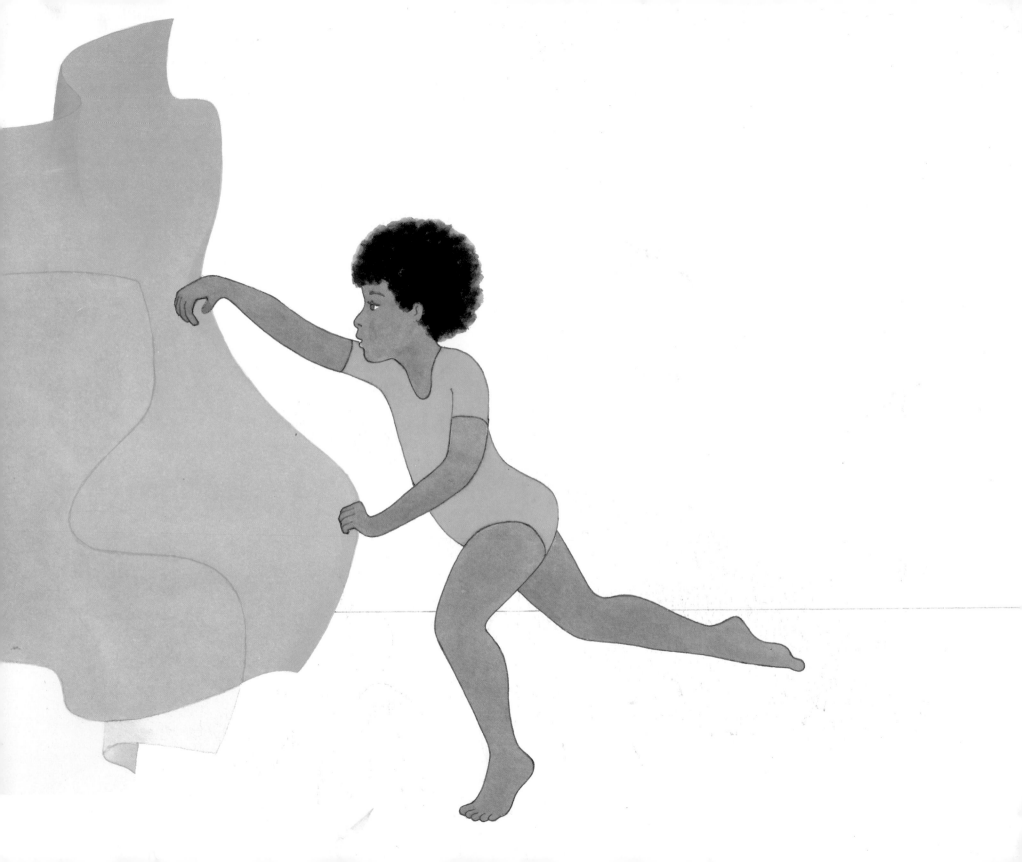

Purple is red and blue mixed together.

No yellow.

Red and red can only make reds.

Yellow and blue can make
chartreuse
and green
and aquamarine.

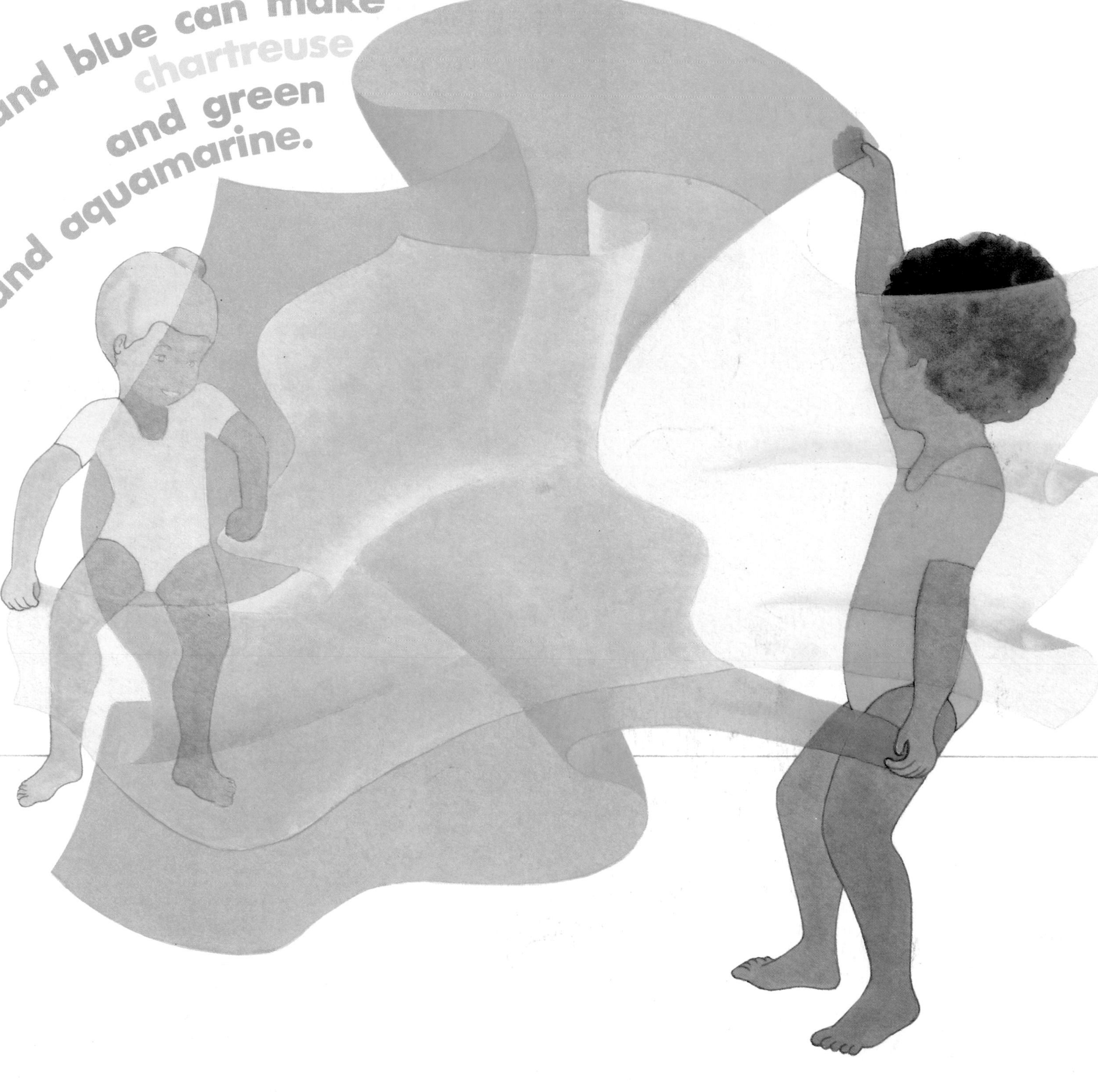

Red and blue can make magenta and purple and violet.

But yellow
and yellow
can only make
yellows.

Blue and blue can only make blues.

But yellow and red can make
marigold
and orange
and vermilion.

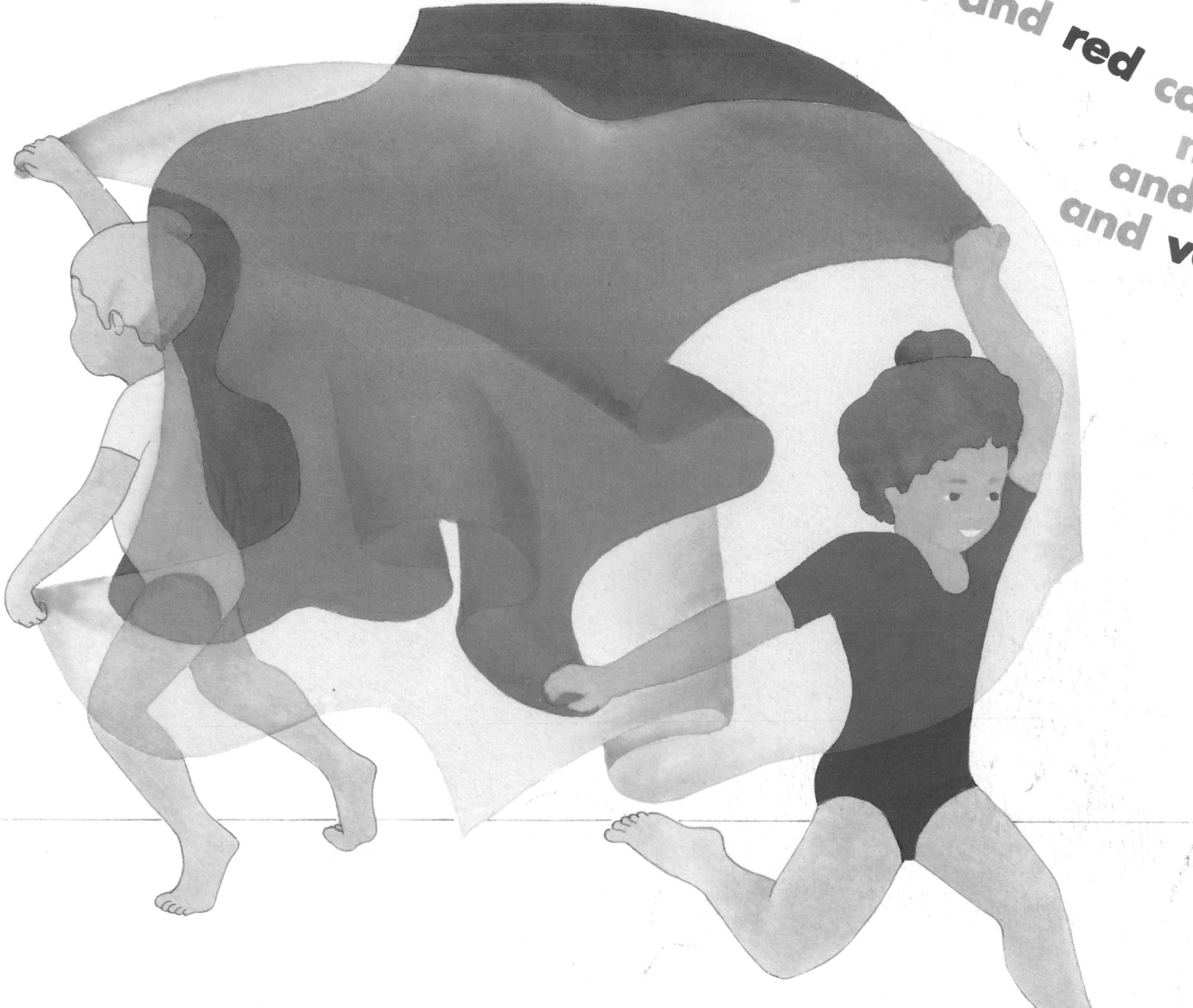

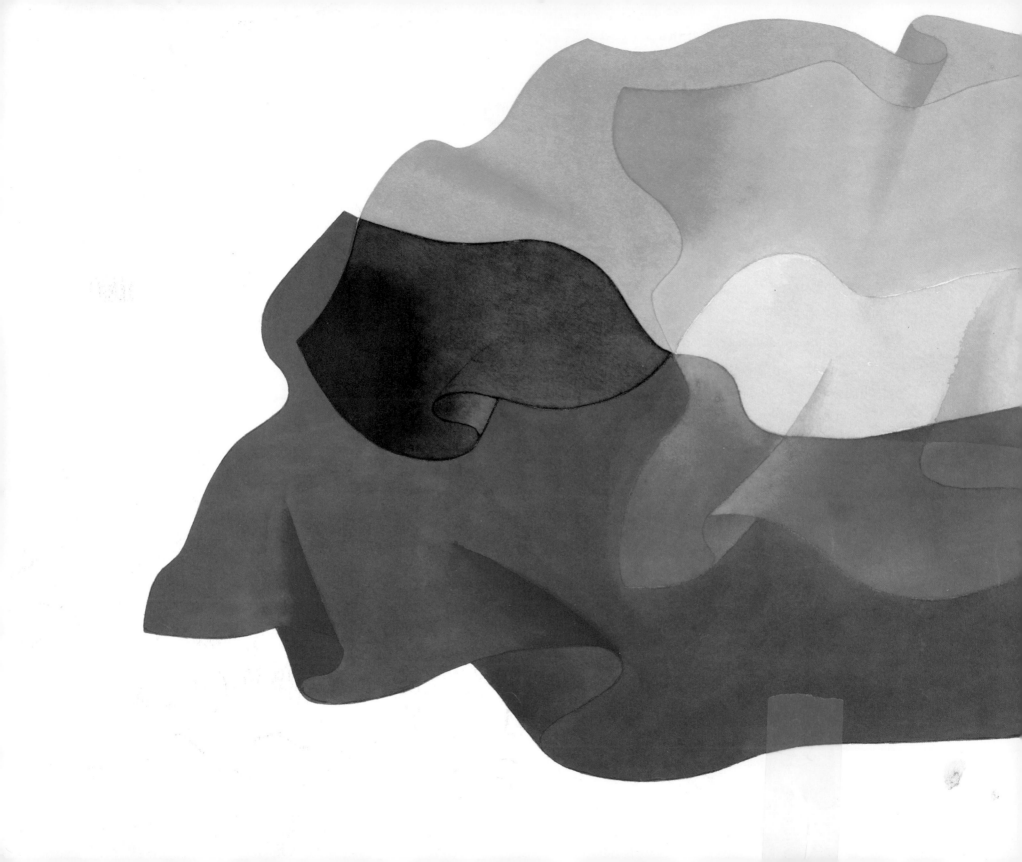

Blue
aquamarine
green
chartreuse!

Yellow
marigold
orange
vermilion!

Red
magenta
purple
violet!

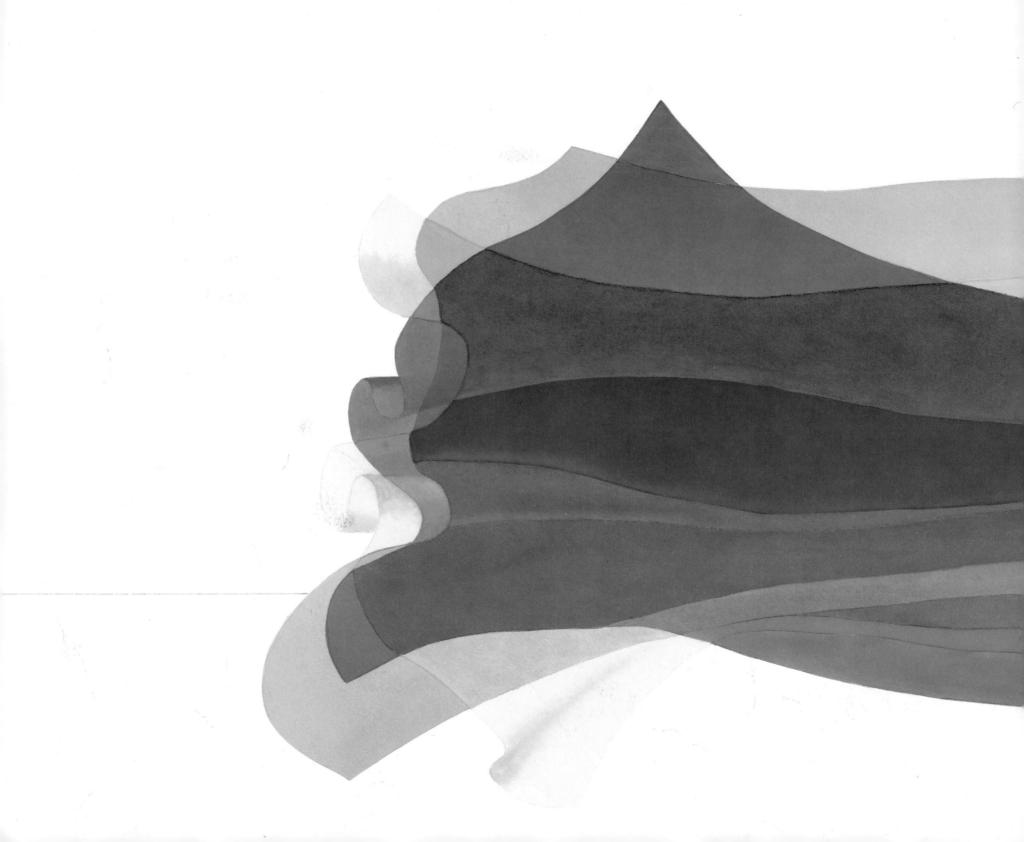

Mix them all together and they make browns and grays.

White makes colors pale.

Gray makes them dark.

Black makes them almost **disappear!**

Color Dance is a fantasy, easier to perform on paper than on a stage. The cleanest mixed colors will be obtained by using pure primary colors—those that do not not contain any of the other primaries. For example, a red with no noticeable blue or yellow in it will produce an equally vibrant orange or purple when mixed with yellow or blue.

The color wheel below shows the relationships between colors. The primary colors (red, yellow, and blue) are equally spaced around the wheel. Halfway between them are the secondary colors (orange, green, and purple). Between the primary and secondary colors are the combinations of adjacent colors, the tertiary colors. Complementary colors are directly opposite one another. Since mixing all three primary colors will produce brown, gray, or black, so will mixing complementary colors, because a pair of complementaries contains all the primaries.

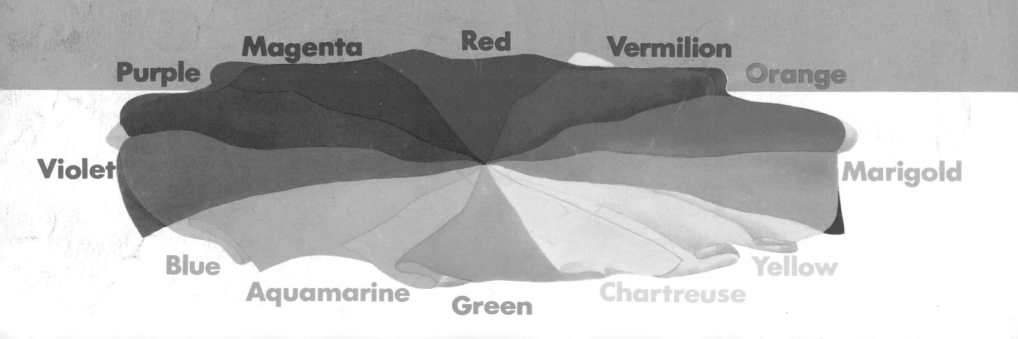

Purple Magenta Red Vermilion Orange

Violet Marigold

Blue Aquamarine Green Chartreuse Yellow